The Path of
Finn
McCool

White Wolves Series Consultant: Sue Ellis,
Centre for Literacy in Primary Education

This book can be used in the White Wolves Guided Reading programme
to help less confident readers in Year 5 gain more independence

First published 2004 by
A & C Black Publishers Ltd
37 Soho Square, London, W1D 3QZ

www.acblack.com

ISBN 0-7136-6842-3

A CIP catalogue for this book is available from the British Library.

A&C Black uses paper produced with elemental chlorine-free
pulp, harvested from managed sustained forests.

Printed and bound in Spain by G. Z. Printek, Bilbao.

The Path of
Finn McCool

retold by Sally Prue
illustrated by Dee Shulman

A & C Black • London

For Dad

Contents

Chapter One

If you go to Ireland, and you catch the 172 bus to Ballycastle, then you'll get to one of the very strangest places in the world.

There by the sea you'll find the Giant's Causeway.

And you'll hardly be able to believe your eyes at the sight of it.

The Giant's Causeway

A great wide path of black stones, it is, all cut with straight sides to them, and fitting together as snug as a honeycomb.

And where does the path go? It goes straight out from the shore and down under the waves of the Irish Sea.

Now, you'll be wondering why anyone should build a path that doesn't go anywhere. But if you have a boat, and you feel like an adventure, you can sail across the sea to Staffa in

Scotland – and there you'll find the other end of the path coming up out on to the land again.

And each stone is so heavy that there's never been any man alive strong enough to lift it.

Now, this is the story of how the path was made, and why most of the stones are under the sea. So that now you need a boat to get to Scotland.

It happened long ago, in the times when there were giants and little

people living in Ireland.

Now, the giants were good people. They were very handy if you wanted your house moved so you had a better view, or so you could put a river between you and your relations. In fact, the giants gave little trouble except for one terrible big, boasting fellow who was called Finn McCool.

Finn McCool was fifty-two feet and six inches tall, and the little people were always having to run for

their lives when he came clumping along, not looking where he was going.

Now, this giant was lucky enough to have a wife and a baby. The baby was a sweet child, not much more than seventeen feet long, and luckily taking after its mother. Finn's wife was called Oona, and the only silly thing she'd ever done in her life was to marry Finn McCool. Many was the time the little people would come knocking at her door, complaining

because Finn had knocked bits off their houses with his great clumsy feet, or spoiled their music with his singing, which sounded like the north wind with bellyache. And then Oona, who was a kind, sensible woman, would bake them a cake the size of a dance floor to cheer them up – and she would tell Finn to watch where he was going.

Now, there came a day when the little people had visitors from Scotland, so they decided to hold a

party to celebrate.

"Now, you stay away," said Oona to Finn. "They won't want you trampling about with your great big feet. Go to the forest and pull up some trees for the fire."

Well, Finn didn't like being told what to do, even though Oona had more brains in her little finger than Finn had in his whole head.

"No one's stopping *me* going to the party," he said to himself. "I'll

show *them* what dancing should really look like!"

The thump-thump-thump of the little people's band could be heard halfway to Scotland, and all the seagulls were sitting with their wings pulled up over their ears, but Finn hopped along in a fine mood.

He stood up on the hill above the place where the little people were having their party.

And he began to dance.

Chapter Two

Now, Finn was not the daintiest person you could find. In fact, you could look about you for a month and not find such a clod-hopping oaf as him. He began to jump up and down on the hill, and the little people began to think there was a thunderstorm on its way. So they took themselves into

the food tent to find some ice cream and some fairy cakes.

But up on the hill, Finn McCool kept on with his hopping and bopping. He jumped and thumped and shook the ground so hard that the tent pegs juddered their way loose and the whole tent came down on the little people's heads.

Well, the little people crawled out of the tent, all rumpled and squashed, with bits of ice cream sticking out of

their ears.

"Idiot!" they shouted. "Oaf! Clumsy great clot!"

The chief of the Scottish little people was especially angry. He was so angry that he climbed a tree until he came right up to Finn's belly button.

"You're a great fool, Finn McCool!" he bellowed.

Now, that was exactly what Oona was going to say when she heard what had happened, only she was going to

say it twenty times louder. But Finn McCool didn't see why he should take it from anyone else.

"I'm the biggest giant in Ireland!" he shouted back. "So I can do what I like!"

"You may be a giant," bawled the chief of the Scottish little people, "but you're not nearly as big as Benan Donner in Scotland. He's a real giant for you. He can throw a cow right over a mountain with his little finger."

Now, Finn McCool didn't like the idea that there might be a bigger giant than him at all. Every day after that he kept thinking about Benan Donner, and in the end he couldn't stand it any longer. He decided he had to go to Scotland to find out for sure who was the biggest.

But he knew he'd have to do it without Oona finding out, or he'd never hear the last of it.

"Oona, my sweet pretty love," he

said one day. "Why don't you take yourself away for a nice holiday to see your sister, and take the baby with you?"

Now, Oona was no fool, and she knew Finn McCool was up to something straight away. She put her hands on her hips and wondered what it was. She decided to take the dear baby to her sister's house, and then sneak back to see what Finn was up to.

34

So Oona put one shawl round her shoulders, and wrapped the baby in another, and off they went. And as soon as they had gone over the hill Finn McCool picked up a hammer the size of a house and bounded down to the shore.

And there he began to build a path to Scotland.

Chapter Three

Now, Finn had a big head, and inside it was mostly empty space, but that didn't mean he couldn't use a hammer. He raised the hammer high in the air and he brought it down on the rocks of the cliff.

SMASH!

The rock split into long columns

with fine straight sides, all ready to be dropped into the sea.

It was hot and heavy work, but Finn split the rocks and then put them together again so they fitted as snug as a honeycomb. Soon there was the beginning of a fine black path reaching out across the sea. The sound of his hammer echoed throughout the land, and shook the gannets off Ailsa Crag, but Finn carried on working. He worked night

and day until the sweat dropped off his nose, and when dawn came up on the third day he could see the misty mountains of Scotland.

And after that he worked even faster.

On the other side of Ireland, at her sister's house, Oona McCool tucked the baby into its cradle, gave him his rattle that was made out of the ribcage of an ox, and tied her shawl back around her shoulders.

45

"You're a good sister to look after the baby for me," she said. "I won't be long, but I have to get back to see what that good-for-nothing husband of mine is up to. I hope the dear baby won't be any trouble."

"Of course not," said the baby's aunt. "I'll let him wrestle with the bull when he wakes up. He'll like that, for sure."

But when Oona got home there was no sign of Finn at all. There was

only a sound like thunder, a long way away across the sea.

So Oona made herself a nice cup of tea and waited to see what would happen.

Finn had never worked so hard in all his life, but there at last was Scotland before him, all fine little islands and air that danced with midges. By lunchtime he came out on to the shore. He jumped up the nearest cliff in two strides of his great knobbly

legs and went off in search of the giant Benan Donner.

Now, Finn was walking along by a lake when he heard a terrible thumping and banging and the ground shivered under his feet.

"That must be thunder," he said to himself.

It got louder and louder, but there was no rain at all.

"Scotland is a strange place," he said, because in Ireland it rains

whenever it gets the chance.

And then over the hill Finn saw something coming. At first it looked like a big haystack; but then it got bigger, and longer, until it blotted out a good bit of the sky.

And then all of a sudden Finn realised that it was the biggest head he had ever seen.

Well, Finn let out a squawk and jumped right into the lake. He lay down in the cold water with just his

eyes and his nose poking out among the reeds.

The great creature was still coming closer. On the end of its huge shoulders grew arms like tree trunks, and on the end of the arms like tree trunks hung the biggest, toughest, most knobbly fists Finn had ever seen.

Benan Donner, the giant.

Benan Donner had muscles all over him. When Benan Donner walked, his body was so hard that it

creaked – but you could hardly hear the creaking, because his footsteps were loud enough to burst your eardrums. Behind him, he left a line of holes where his weight had split the rocks.

Now, Finn had a big head, and what was inside was mostly wind, but he was out of the lake and running as fast as he could the moment Benan Donner was out of sight.

And in less time than it takes to tell, he was running back along his beautiful black path all the way to Ireland.

Chapter Four

Finn McCool didn't stop running until he was in his own house. Oona was there, mixing up some cake in a bowl the size of a bathtub. Finn stood, and he panted and groaned and gasped.

"What's the matter?" asked Oona, breaking three dozen eggs into the bowl with a flick of her wrist.

"I'm going to die!" said Finn. "I've been all the way to Scotland, and there's a giant there called Benan Donner. And he has muscles so big he could throw *me* over the mountain!"

"Well, never mind," said Oona. "That needn't bother us, for he's a long way away. There's no boat in the world that'd hold a great hulk like him, and we can be quite sure he'll never learn to fly."

But Finn sat down and shook his head.

"He doesn't need a boat," he said. "Because I've built a path across the sea all the way to Scotland."

And at that moment there came a low rumbling from over the sea. It sounded like thunder, but Finn knew what it was. It was the footsteps of the very biggest giant of all.

"I'm going to die!" moaned Finn, again.

"Oh, calm yourself, Finn," said Oona, and carried on making her cakes. She made the mixture and poured half of it into a tin the size of a cartwheel. Then she did the same with the rest, except that into the middle of this cake she put the iron griddle she used when she made scones.

The thunder was getting closer and closer. Oona opened the iron door above the fireplace and put the cakes in the oven.

"I'm going to die," said Finn. "Benan Donner will pull my head off and use it for a football. He'll gnaw my bones. He'll make buttons of my toenails."

"Nonsense," said Oona. "You've forgotten all about your secret weapon."

Finn stared at her.

"Have I got a secret weapon?" he asked, hopefully.

"Oh yes," said Oona, and she

fetched two nice clean sheets and her best petticoat. "Now, roll up your trousers, Finn McCool, and show me your knobbly knees."

Oona pinned one sheet to the front of Finn McCool, and the other behind him. Then she tied her petticoat around his head. Finn looked the biggest fool in Ireland, but he was so scared that he didn't say a word.

"Now, jump into the baby's cradle," said Oona. "For Benan

67

Donner is coming up the path."

So Finn McCool jumped into the baby's cradle and pulled the covers up to his nose. Now, Finn was fifty-two feet six inches tall, and the baby was barely seventeen feet, even though he was a fine baby that could drain a cow dry for breakfast. Finn's hairy legs stuck out at the bottom of the cradle, and his great knobbly fingers clutched at the blanket, and his eyes were so wide with terror they were as big as millstones.

And no sooner was he all tucked up than there came a BANG BANG BANG! on the door of the house.

And at the third bang the door fell off its hinges and Benan Donner stood there, as tall as a cliff and twice as ugly.

Chapter Five

"Where's Finn?" Benan Donner bellowed, as loud as a hurricane.

"Was that Finn McCool you were wanting?" asked Oona, putting the cakes on the table. They smelt like heaven, and Benan Donner licked his lips with a tongue the size of a ham and took a step inside. "Finn McCool,

the biggest giant in Ireland? Because you won't find him here today."

"The little people told me he lives here," Benan Donner roared. "I'm going to bash his head, and mash the rest of him into rissoles!"

"Well, in that case you'd better come right in," said Oona.

So Benan Donner took another step into the room, and he was so ugly that Finn couldn't help but let out a yelp of terror.

"Ah," said Oona, fondly. "The little baby must be hungry, poor thing."

And she gave one cake to Finn McCool, and the other to Benan Donner.

Well, Benan Donner took hold of his cake with both hands and he opened his mouth as wide as a church door. Then he took a great bite out of it with his big teeth.

CLANG!

"Owwwwwwwwwww!" howled Benan

Donner, with his mouth full of iron and his eyes spinning like windmills.

"Oh dear," said Oona. "That cake's not too hard for you, is it, Mr Donner? Because I could give it a soak in some milk for you, like I do for my poor old mother."

But Benan Donner was as big-headed as Finn was. In fact, some of the time, he was worse.

"No cake's too hard for me," he blustered, grinding his teeth. Two of

them fell out, but he spat them into the corner.

"I thought it couldn't be," said Oona, "for that's the special soft cake that I bake for the baby, bless him."

Now, Benan Donner tried not to look at babies if he could avoid it. But now he looked across at the cradle – and his eyes nearly popped out.

"That's the ugliest baby ever!" he shouted. For the baby had a great bulb of a nose, and the knobbliest

knees Benan Donner had ever seen.

"Sure, and he takes after his father," said Oona, proudly.

Benan Donner looked at the baby some more. The baby had big knobbly hands and big knobbly feet and a whole mat of hairs on its chest. And it was eating its cake with no trouble at all.

Now, Benan Donner's big head was mostly full of air, but he wasn't as stupid as all that.

If Finn McCool's baby was that big, and that strong, and that ugly, then what was his father like?

Well, Benan Donner was out of that house and halfway to the shore faster than I can tell you.

And by the time Finn had heaved himself out of the cradle, Benan Donner was racing back across Finn McCool's path to Scotland just as fast as his great hairy legs would take him. And, just to be on the safe side,

Benan Donner pulled up lots of the stones as he went and threw them into the sea, where they made a new island, which today is called the Isle of Man.

And so, from that very day, Finn McCool was the biggest giant in Ireland again. But if ever Finn got too bossy, or too big-headed, or too careless about where he put his big flat feet, then Oona would take him down to the shore and show him the

beginning of the path he'd made.

And when Finn McCool thought about Benan Donner he would stop being big-headed at once. He'd go and pull up a couple of rose bushes as a present for Oona, who was his secret weapon, or else he'd take some of the little people for a nice ride round Ireland in a basket.

Now, that all happened long, long ago. But if you go to Ireland, and take the number 172 bus to Ballycastle,

you can still see the great black stones of the beginning of the path Finn McCool made. And if you go to Staffa, in Scotland, you can see the other end, too, at a place called Fingal's Cave. And, sure as I'm telling you, there's the Isle of Man, as large as life, just where Benan Donner threw all the rest of Finn's stones into the sea.

And it was all of it done by the biggest giant in Ireland.

About the Author

Sally Prue has lived in Hertfordshire since she was adopted as a baby. She went to local schools and then started work in the paper mill at the end of the road. She left work to look after her two daughters, and took the opportunity of being at home to play lots of music. Now she works as a piano and recorder teacher and is also one of the most exciting new writers for young people. Her first novel, *Cold Tom*, won the Smarties Silver Award and the Branford Boase Award.

Another White Wolves title you might enjoy ...

The Barber's Clever Wife
by Narinder Dhami

Many years ago, there lived a lazy barber who kept losing customers by cutting them and *not* their hair! Luckily, he had a clever wife with cunning plans to earn the couple money. But was she smart enough to fool the thieves?

Another White Wolves title you might enjoy ...

Taliesin
by Maggie Pearson

A boy drinks from the magic cauldron of knowledge and is reborn as Taliesin – magician, prophet and trickster. Now he has the power to change the fortunes of all he encounters – for better and for worse ...

White Wolves